3 2113 00607 2196

D0624992

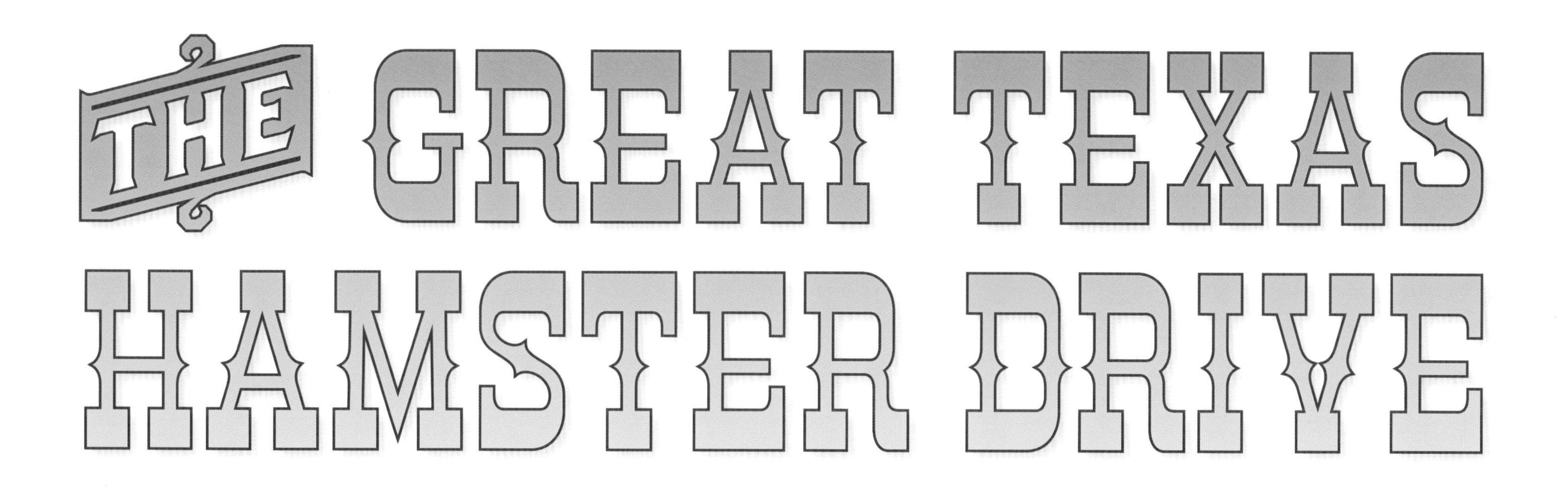

by Eric A. Kimmel illustrated by Bruce Whatley

Marshall Cavendish Children

The idea for this story came from Sheila Gauntt, the librarian at Cooper Elementary School in Georgetown, Texas. Sheila told me about her neighbor who had a commercial hamster breeding business in his barn. Sheila, her children, and all the kids in the neighborhood worked there at one time taking care of thousands of hamsters. That started me thinking: Texas, ranch, hamsters, cowboys. The story began to flow.

Marshall Cavendish Corporation, 99 White Plains Road, Tarrytown, NY 10591
www.marshallcavendish.us/kids

Library of Congress Cataloging-in-Publication Data
Kimmel, Eric A.
The great Texas hamster drive: an original tall tale / by Eric A. Kimmel; illustrated by Bruce Whatley.—1st ed.
p. cm.
Summary: When Pecos Bill's daughter gets two pet hamsters, they soon multiply into the hundreds, so Bill decides to take them all to Chicago where lots of boys and girls want pet hamsters.
ISBN 978-0-7614-5357-4
[1. Hamsters—Fiction. 2. West (U.S.)—History—Fiction. 3. Tall tales.] I. Whatley, Bruce, ill. II. Title. III. Title: Original tall tale.
PZ7.K5648Gr 2007
[E]—dc22
2006039521

The text of this book is set in Barbera.
The illustrations are rendered in watercolor.
Book design by Becky Terhune
Editor: Margery Cuyler

Printed in China
First edition
1 3 5 6 4 2

To Sheila Gauntt and the children
of Cooper Elementary School
—E. A. K.

For Sela Rose
—B. W.

IF YOU'VE HEARD about Pecos Bill, then you surely know about his gal, Slue Foot Sue. No doubt you've heard the story of how Sue tried to ride Bill's horse, Widow Maker, and how she ended up on the moon. It took Bill three weeks to get her down, and when he did, Sue was so mad, she didn't talk to him for a month.

But they worked it out. Soon after that they got married and settled down on a big ranch in Texas. They raised kids and longhorns.

Four were boys (the kids, that is): Bob, Ben, Bart, and Beau.

The fifth was a gal, Slue Foot Sal. Sal was a tiny little thing. She barely came up to her brothers' belt buckles. But she ran the house. If Sal wanted something, she got it.

One evening at dinner Sal announced, "I want a pet. Bob, Ben, Bart, and Beau have pets. I want one, too."

"What kind of pet do you want, honey?" Sue asked.

"How about a timber wolf," said Ben, reaching for the potatoes.

"A rattler'd suit her better," said Bob, which drew a stern look from his parents.

"Here's what I want," said Sal. She showed everyone a picture of a little animal.

"That looks like a mouse," said Bill. "If you want a pet mouse, go to the barn. We got plenty of 'em there."

"It's not a mouse, Daddy," Sal said. "It's a hamster. Hamsters have cheek pouches and short little tails. Isn't it the cutest thing?"

"Where can we get one?" Sue asked.

"I know," said Bill. "I'll give Ike Levy a call." Bill had known Ike when Ike was a peddler driving his wagon down the back roads of West Texas. Now he owned the biggest mail-order house in the country.

Bill cranked up the telephone the next morning and made a call to Chicago.

"Bill, you old sidewinder, it's good to hear your voice. What can I do for you?" Ike said when he came on the phone.

"You got any hamsters?" Bill asked.

"If they're in the catalog, I got 'em. Page eight seventy-six. Cute little things. How many do you want?"

"Just one will be fine," said Bill. "Sal wants a pet."

"I'll send two," said Ike. "One might get lonely."

A week later the Railway Express wagon pulled up to the ranch. "Package for Miss Slue Foot Sal," the deliveryman said. Sal couldn't wait to open it.

"Ain't they cute!" Sal exclaimed as she showed everybody her new hamsters.

"Looks like mice to me. Don't we got enough mice already?" Cookie muttered.

"Button your lip and smile," Bill warned.

Cookie and the other cowboys started grinning. "They sure are sweet, Miss Sally!"

Sal named her hamsters Crockett and Bowie, after Texas's two great heroes. She should have named one Alice or Dinah, because soon there were five hamsters. Then fifteen. Then twenty-eight hamsters. Bill, Bob, Ben, Bart, and Beau had to keep building bigger and bigger cages to hold them all.

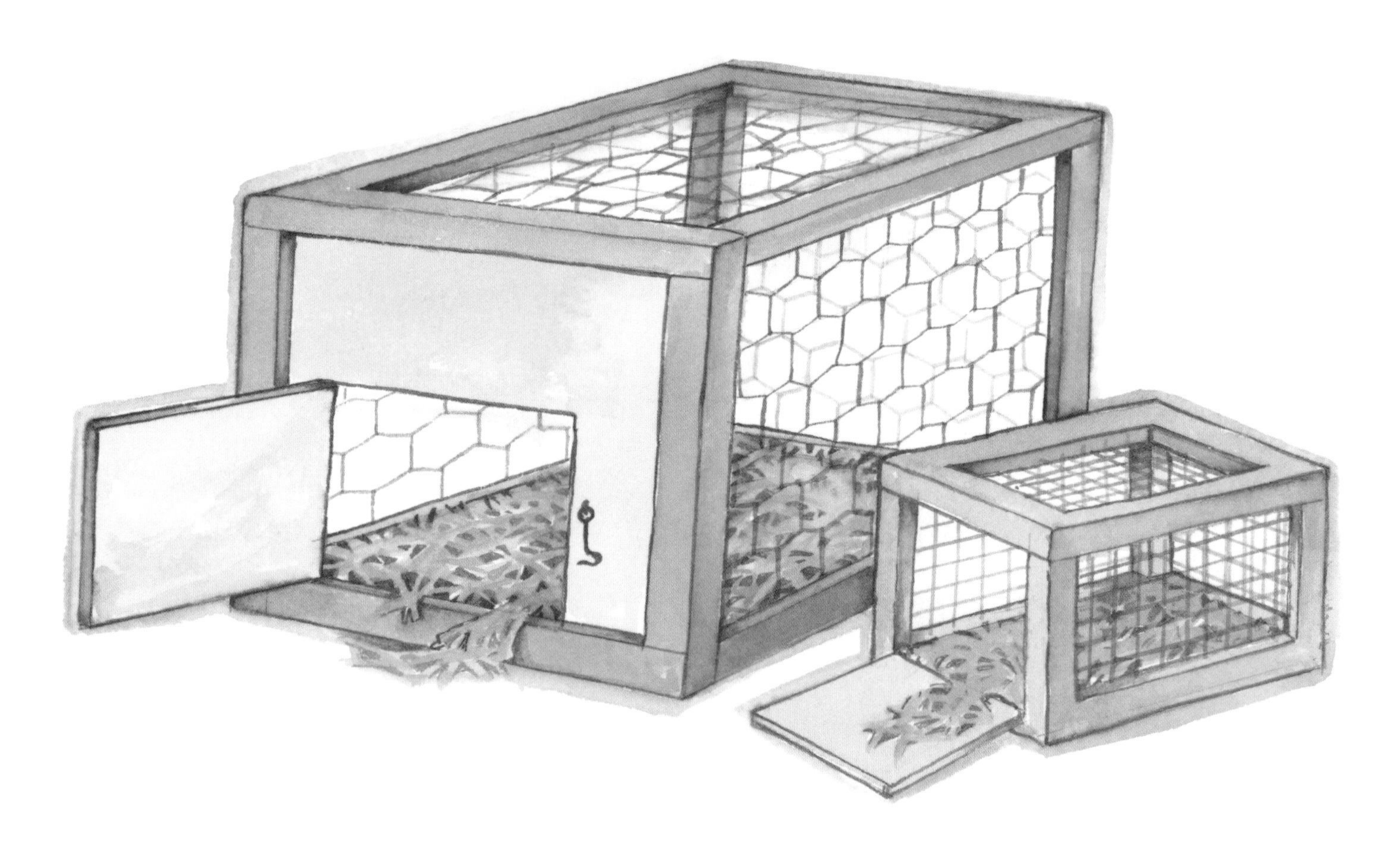

One terrible day Sal came home from school. She let out a shriek. The cage doors were open. The hamsters were gone.

"Don't cry, Sal," her brothers said. "We'll find 'em."

They searched all over the house, all over the ranch, all over the prairie. The hamsters were gone.

"Coyotes must've got 'em. Or maybe owls," said Cookie.

He was wrong.

Hamsters began appearing on the range. Bill's cowboys sighted a few at first, then more and more. The hamsters began running in packs, hundreds of 'em. They ate all the grass. They drove the longhorns away from the water holes.

"We gotta do something, Bill!" the cowboys said.

Bill got on the phone to Ike. "You gotta help me. These critters are taking over my ranch."

"How many you got?" Ike asked.

"Three or four thousand. Tomorrow I may have eight or nine," said Bill.

"Round 'em all up, take 'em to Abilene, and put them on the railroad to Chicago. City kids love hamsters. They can't have dogs or cats in those little apartments, but hamsters do fine. I'll find a good home for every one you send me."

The Great Texas Hamster Drive began the next morning. Everybody on the ranch spent days in the saddle, rounding up hamsters.

"I think we got all of 'em," Bill finally said.

"I hope so," said Sue.

“Head ’em up! Move ’em out!” cried Bill at dawn on the tenth of June. Eighteen thousand, three hundred and seventy-six hamsters started out on the trail to Abilene, herded along by Sal, her brothers, and eight wranglers. Cookie rode behind them in the chuck wagon. Sue stayed home to keep an eye on things.

Every day brought new challenges. They had to keep an eye out for hawks and owls as well as coyotes and prairie wolves. Getting the herd across a river was some challenge, too. Hamsters don't swim. Bill and his outfit had to pack 'em in hats, pockets, and saddlebags. Cookie filled every pot and pan in the chuck wagon.

"Dern mice!" he grumbled.

A storm hit in the middle of the night. Lightning cracked. Thunder boomed like cannons. The hamsters started squeaking.

A lightning bolt struck, and they were off.

Stampede!

Sal and the others chased those hamsters for miles, until the storm finally lifted. The hamsters began to slow down. “We got ’em!” yelled Sal. Suddenly all the hamsters disappeared! Every last one! Gone!

“Where’d they go?” everybody wondered.

Sal jumped down from her pony. She walked back and forth, studying the ground. She threw down her hat and stomped on it.

“Dang!” she hollered. “We lost ’em!” Sal pointed to a hole in the ground. And another hole. And another. There were holes everywhere!

“It’s a prairie dog town,” Bill said. “The hamsters went down those prairie dog holes. They’re underground now. How’re we gonna get ’em back?”

“Maybe we can dig ’em out?” Bob and Beau suggested.

Bill shook his head. “You can’t dig a varmint out of a prairie dog town. These towns are the size of some eastern states. The tunnels go on for miles. We’ll just have to camp here and wait. Maybe they’ll come out. Maybe they won’t. I don’t know what else to do.”

Nobody had a better idea. So they squatted around the prairie dog holes in the middle of that vast prairie dog town, hoping that sooner or later, the hamsters might come out.

That's what they were doing when Cookie rode in on the chuck wagon. It had taken him nearly all day to catch up with them.

"What're you fellers doin'?" he asked.

"The hamsters ran down into a prairie dog town," Bob told him. "We're waiting for them to come out."

"Dagnabbit!" Cookie hollered. "Here's how you get critters out of a prairie dog town." He opened the back of the chuck wagon and took the stovepipe off his little cookstove. He carried it over to a prairie dog hole and stuck it into the ground.

"What's that supposed to do?" Ben asked.
"Wait and see," said Cookie.

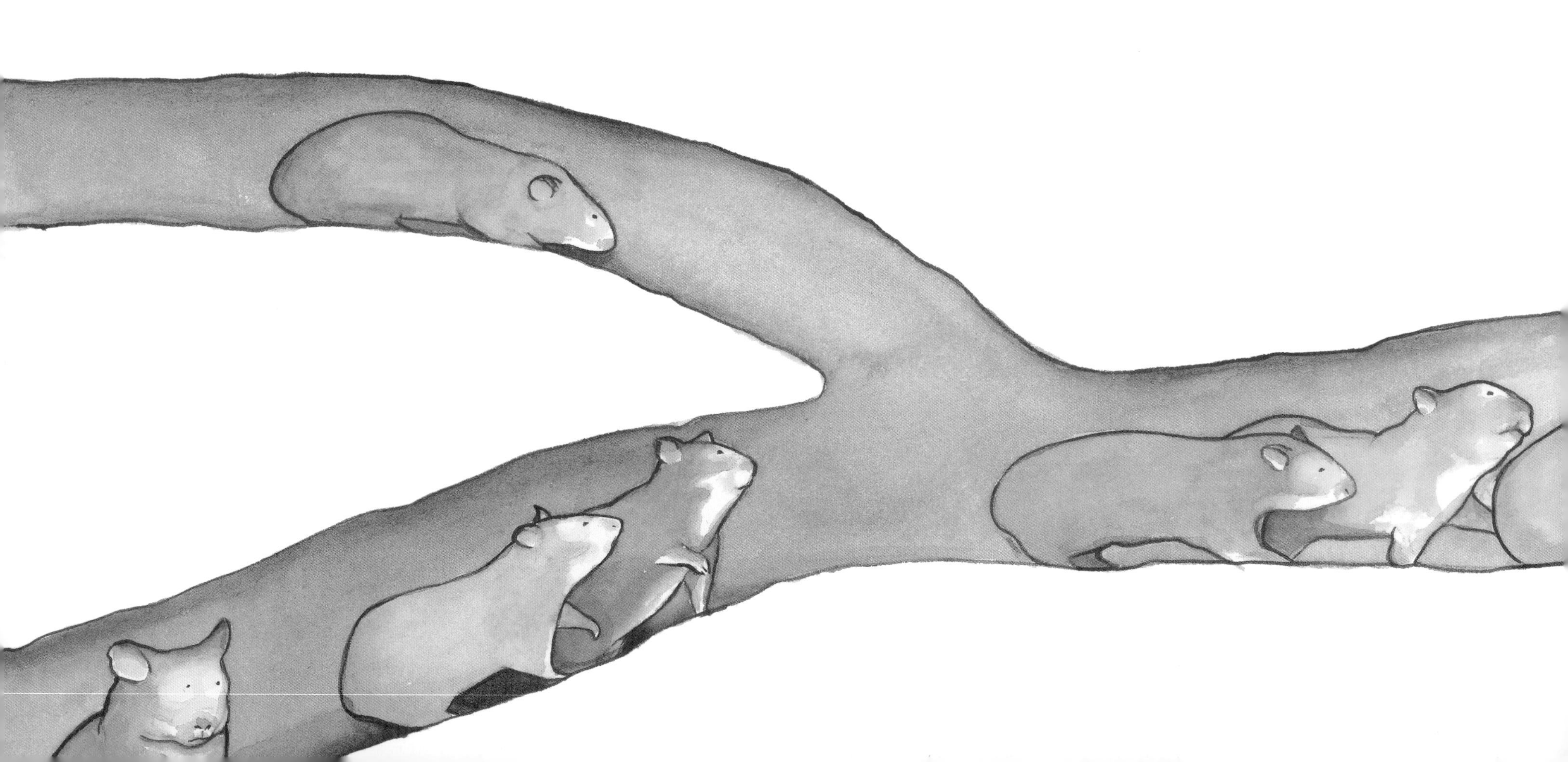

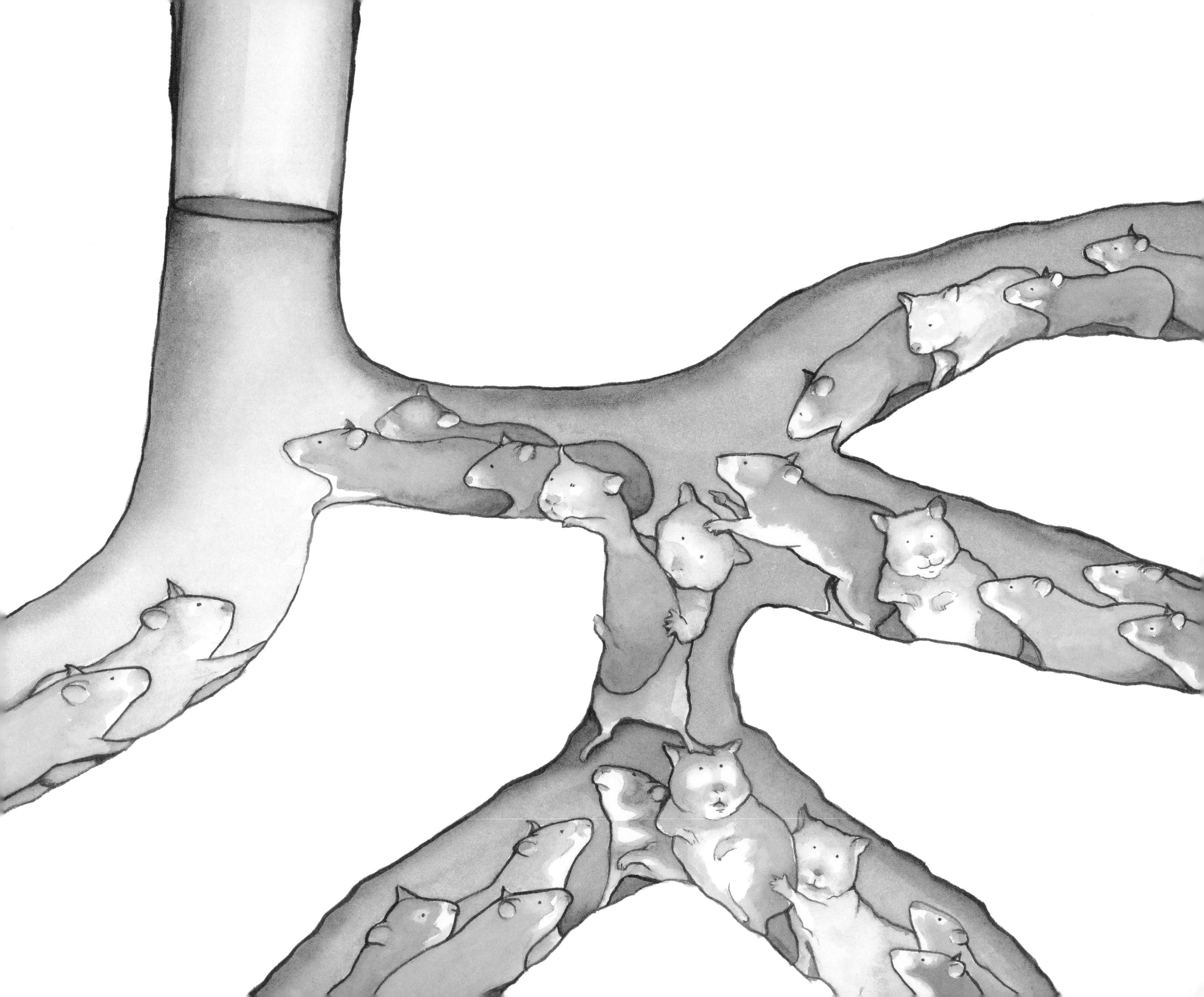

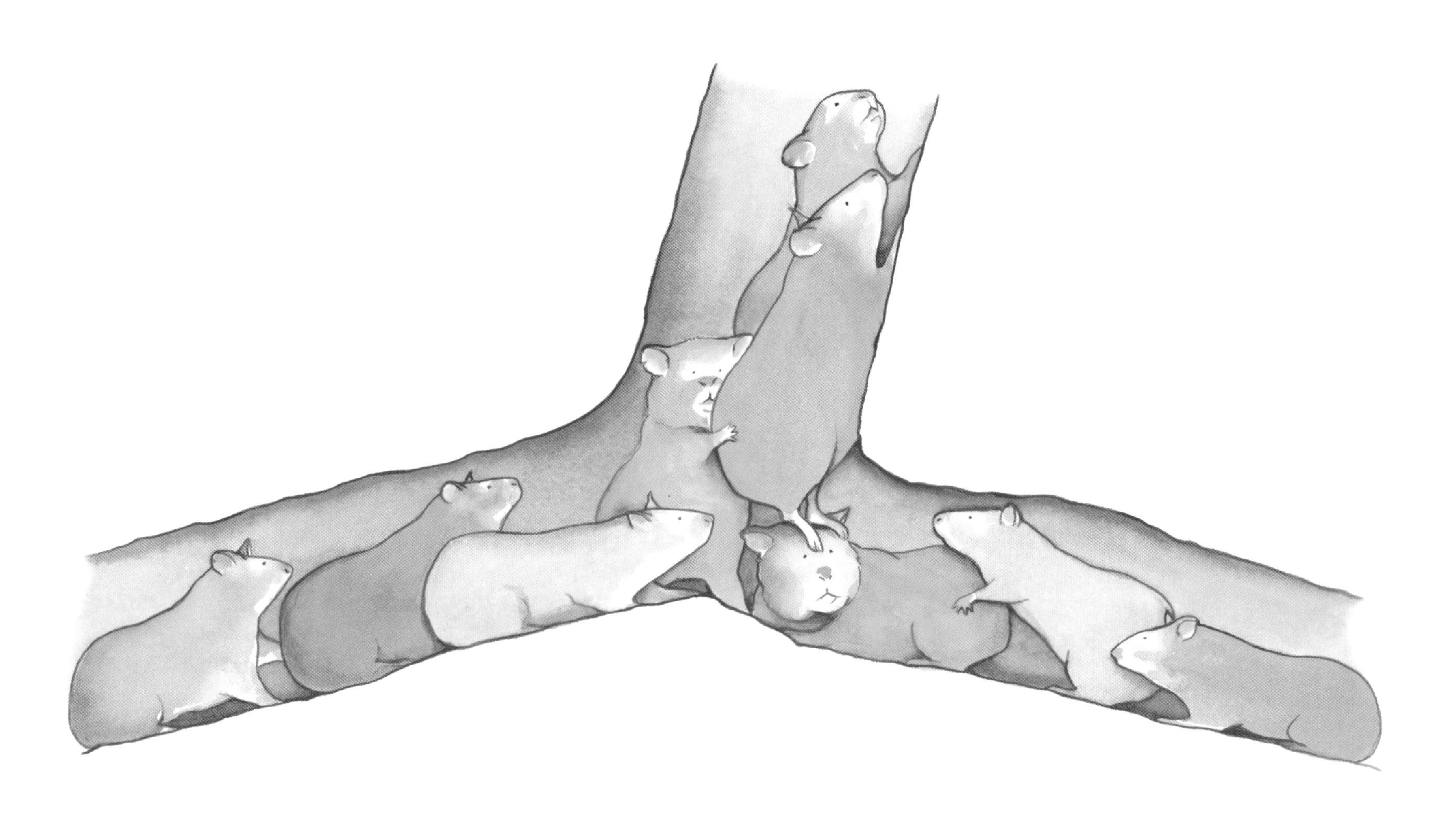

Suddenly they heard a rumble coming from deep below. The ground began to shake. "It's an earthquake!" Bart yelled.

"It ain't no earthquake," said Cookie. "It's hamsters!"

The hamsters came boiling up from the prairie dog town, up through the tunnels, up through the stovepipe. Within minutes, the whole herd was back.

"I don't care what you call 'em: hamsters, rats, or mice," Cookie said. "If you want to get those critters out of a tunnel, give 'em another tunnel to explore."

It didn't take long to sort out the herd and get back on the trail. They made it to Abilene without any more fuss.

Everybody—especially Sal—felt their heart-strings tugging as they loaded the hamsters into the boxcars. Trains would take them to Chicago and from there all over the country. Maybe even all over the world. Wherever Ike's catalog went, hamsters would follow.

Sal couldn't help feeling teary-eyed, knowing she was saying good-bye to Crockett, Bowie, Houston, Austin, Alice, Dinah, and all the rest. But when she thought about all the big city boys and girls who needed something small and cuddly to care for, she felt a whole lot better. She knew her little pals would be happy in their new homes.

But when the train pulled out, Sal started crying again.

"What's the matter, honey?" Bill asked.

"I don't have a pet anymore. Not even one!" Sal wailed.

"We'll find you some new pets," Bill promised.

"Snakes are fun," said Bob and Ben, "as long as they don't have rattles."

"We'll catch you some horny toads," said Bart and Beau.

"How about a crow?" Cookie suggested. "You can teach crows tricks. I once had a pet crow that was smarter than me."

"I already know what I want," said Sal. She whispered something in Bill's ear.

"You bet, honey. We'll look in the mail-order catalog. I'll bet Ike can get some for you." Bill leaned over and whispered to Cookie, "What're gerbils?"

"You'll find out," Cookie answered.

He sure did!